This
Treasure Cove Story
belongs to

THE PRINCE AND THE PAUPER

A CENTUM BOOK 978-1-911460-57-2
Published in Great Britain by Centum Books Ltd.
This edition published 2021.

1 3 5 7 9 10 8 6 4 2

Centum Books Ltd, 20 Devon Square, Newton Abbot, Devon, TQ12 2HR, UK.
9/10 Fenian St, Dublin 2, D02 RX24, Ireland.

www.centumbooksltd.co.uk | books@centumbooksltd.co.uk
CENTUM BOOKS Limited Reg. No. 07641486.

A CIP catalogue record for this book is available
from the British Library.

Printed in China.

A Treasure Cove Story

DISNEY'S

THE PRINCE AND THE PAUPER

Adapted by Fran Manushkin

Illustrated by Russel Shroeder and Don Williams

Once upon a time there was a good and kindly
king. He ruled his country with fairness and
generosity.

But one day the king became very ill and could
no longer watch over his kingdom. His son, the
prince, worried by his father's bedside.

'Aha,' said the greedy captain of the guards. 'Now my friends and I can steal from all the king's subjects!' And day after day they filled up the palace with mountains of food and trunks of gold.

It seemed that nobody could save the kingdom from the thieving captain. Then one day…

...two peasants hoping to find something to eat wandered near the palace.

It just happened that one of the paupers, Mickey, looked exactly like the king's son, the prince. But this beggar boy's life was not like the life of the prince. Mickey had no fine clothes to wear nor a fancy palace to live in. But he did have two loyal friends. One was a bumbling fellow named Goofy, and the other was a large, friendly dog named Pluto.

Mickey and Goofy watched as the captain of the guards sped by in the royal coach. 'Look at those delicious turkey drumsticks,' sighed Mickey.

'Woof, woof,' barked the hungry Pluto as he chased the coach towards the palace.

'Stop!' shouted Mickey. 'Come back!' He dashed away after the dog.

Pluto chased the royal coach to the gates of the
palace, with Mickey right behind him. To Mickey's
suprise, the royal guard waved him in – and called
him 'Your Majesty'.

'Our prince is certainly dressed oddly today,'
thought the guard. 'And he's got himself a new
dog, too.'

By now, Goofy had lost sight of Mickey and
wondered where he'd disappeared to.

Meanwhile, inside the palace, the real prince was
sitting through a boring lesson. To amuse himself,
he took out his peashooter and aimed it at his servant,
Donald.

'Wak!' shouted Donald when he got hit. He shot
a pea back at the prince. But he missed the prince
and hit the tutor, who tossed him out of the room.

At that moment, all of them heard a loud crash near the palace entrance. They ran to see what the noise was and saw a suit of armour rolling around on the floor.

'I'm sorry,' said a voice inside the armour. 'I guess I got tangled up.'

Then the prince saw a face peering out of the helmet – a face that looked exactly like his! Both the prince and pauper screamed.

After Mickey explained who he was, the prince took him into his room so they could have a talk.

'Oh,' sighed the prince, 'how happy your life must be. You never have to take any boring lessons and you can wander and play all day.'

'But you go to feasts all the time,' said Mickey, whose empty stomach was growling.

'I have a wonderful idea,' said the prince. 'Why don't you and I change places for a day?'

Mickey hesitated. 'I don't think that would work at all. I don't know how to be a prince.'

'Oh, it's easy,' the prince assured him. And soon Mickey and the prince had exchanged clothes.

Then the prince gaily waved good-bye and dashed out the door of the palace. This time, the captain of the guards, seeing a boy who looked like a peasant, angrily booted him and his dog over the wall and into a snowbank.

'Ha,' the prince chuckled, 'My disguise is working. My own guard didn't recognise me!'

But the prince didn't fool Pluto. A quick sniff and a closer look told the dog this boy was not his old friend. Pluto sadly walked away.

'Hey, there you are!' shouted Goofy. 'I've been looking all over for you!'

'Uh, hello!' said the prince. He did not know the pauper's friend and quickly rushed away.

Back at the palace, Donald brought food to
Mickey's room. Mickey, who was very hungry,
reached for it, but Donald snatched it away. 'I'm
checking for poison,' he said biting into a turkey
leg and smacking his lips.

The smell of food was driving Mickey crazy and
he was afraid Donald would eat his entire lunch.
'Thanks,' said Mickey, grabbing the leg back from
Donald. Then he pushed the duck out of the door
and slammed it behind him.

'Now it's time for your falconry lesson,' said the tutor, showing Mickey how to control the bird. But instead of making the falcon fly, the angry bird chased Mickey and made him fly – in the opposite direction!

The horse riding lesson didn't go any better – Mickey kept falling off his horse!

Meanwhile, the real prince had decided to
try sledging through the snow with the peasants.
Unfortunately, he tripped and tumbled down
the hill, becoming a giant snowball!

The prince rolled and rolled down to a busy
marketplace. And there, to his astonishment, the
prince saw the captain of the guards stealing food
from the peasants!

'Stop!' ordered the prince, but the guards didn't
recognise him and kept on stealing. 'I had no idea
our guards were taking food from the people,' said
the prince. 'There'll certainly be some changes when
I get back to the palace.'

Just then a royal food wagon appeared. 'Give these people food,' the prince ordered the guard showing him his royal ring.

'Yes, sir,' said the guard when he saw the ring. But the cruel captain and his men came dashing through the crowd, trying to steal the food back. They shoved the people and the prince as well. Luckily, Goofy came along and helped him to escape.

'You saved my life!' the prince said gratefully.

Just a few minutes later the town crier came by and announced that the good king had died.

'I must go to the palace right away,' said the prince. 'I will miss my father greatly, but now it is my duty to take over as king.'

'Gosh,' said Goofy. 'You're the prince. I didn't know. I thought you were my old buddy Mickey.'

'I am you're friend from now on,' vowed the prince as he rushed away towards the palace.

At the palace, the prince was greeted by the captain
of the guards. 'I see your royal ring,' the captain said.
'But it won't do you any good.' He grabbed the prince
and tossed him in the dungeon. 'As soon as the pauper
is crowned king,' said the captain, 'I shall unmask him
as an impostor and rule the kingdom myself!'

The prince soon discovered that he had company.
Donald was in the dungeon, too.

The prince stared at the locked door. 'If I don't get
out in time for my coronation, our kingdom will be
ruined!'

Just then the door down the hall opened and
a prison guard rushed in. He was a very strange
guard who stumbled and bumped into everyone.
He bumped hardest against the other guard, who
tumbled to the floor.

'Hi, prince,' the guard giggled. It wasn't a guard at all. It was Goofy!

'You saved my life again,' said the prince. Then the prince took out the keys and unlocked the dungeon and everybody dashed out.

Meanwhile, in the throne room, Mickey was trying desperately to wriggle away from the royal crown. 'Please don't put it on my head,' he begged.

'He's not the prince!' yelled the evil captain. 'He's an impostor! Seize him!'

'But I'm not an impostor!' came a voice from the balcony. It was the real prince!

The prince was crowned king and his first act was
to arrest the evil captain and all his scheming friends.
Everybody in the kingdom was happy again
– especially Pluto, who was reunited with his old
friend Mickey.

From that day on, the new king, like his father, ruled with kindness and generosity. He always remembered his day as a pauper and he saw to it that nobody went hungry.

He made Goofy captain of the guards and Mickey became provider of food.

Together they created a wonderful kingdom for all!

Treasure Cove Stories

Please contact Centum Books
to receive the full list of titles in
the *Treasure Cove Stories* series.
books@centumbooksltd.co.uk

1 Three Little Pigs
2 Snow White and
the Seven Dwarfs
3 The Fox and the Hound
- Hide-and-Seek
4 Dumbo
5 Cinderella
6 Cinderella's Friends
7 Alice in Wonderland
8 Mad Hatter's Tea Party
from Alice in Wonderland
9 Mickey Mouse and
his Spaceship
10 Peter Pan
11 Pinocchio
12 Mickey and the Beanstalk
13 Sleeping Beauty
and the Good Fairies
14 The Lucky Puppy
15 Chicken Little
16 The Incredibles
17 Coco
18 Winnie the Pooh and Tigger
19 The Sword in the Stone
20 Mary Poppins
21 The Jungle Book
22 Aristocats
23 Lady and the Tramp
24 Bambi
25 Bambi - Friends of the Forest
26 Pete's Dragon
27 Beauty and the Beast
- The Teapot's Tale
28 Monsters, Inc.
– M is for Monster
29 Finding Nemo
30 The Incredibles 2
31 The Incredibles
– Jack-Jack Attack
33 Wall-E
34 Up
35 The Princess and the Frog
36 Toy Story – The Pet Problem

39 Spider-Man – Night of the Vulture!
40 Wreck it Ralph
41 Ralph Breaks the Internet
42 The Invincible Iron Man
– Eye of the Dragon
45 Toy Story – A Roaring Adventure
46 Cars – Deputy Mater Saves
the Day!
47 Spider-Man – Trapped by the
Green Goblin
49 Spider-Man – High Voltage!
50 Frozen
51 Cinderella is my Babysitter
52 Beauty and the Beast
- I am the Beast
56 I am a Princess
57 The Big Book of Paw Patrol
58 Paw Patrol
- Adventures with Grandpa!
59 Paw Patrol - Pirate Pups!
60 Trolls
61 Trolls Holiday
63 Zootropolis
64 Ariel is my Babysitter
65 Tiana is my Babysitter
66 Belle is my Babysitter
67 Paw Patrol
- Itty-Bitty Kitty Rescue
68 Moana
70 Guardians of the Galaxy
71 Captain America
- High-Stakes Heist!
72 Ant-Man
73 The Mighty Avengers
74 The Mighty Avengers
- Lights Out!
75 The Incredible Hulk
78 Paw Patrol - All-Star Pups!
80 I am Ariel
82 Jasmine is my Babysitter
87 Beauty and the Beast - I am Belle
88 The Lion Guard
- The Imaginary Okapi
89 Thor - Thunder Strike!
90 Guardians of the Galaxy
- Rocket to the Rescue!
93 Olaf's Frozen Adventure
95 Trolls - Branch's Bunker Birthday

96 Trolls - Poppy's Party
97 The Ugly Duckling
98 Cars - Look Out for Mater!
99 101 Dalmatians
100 The Sorcerer's Apprentice
101 Tangled
102 Avengers
– The Threat of Thanos
105 The Mighty Thor
106 Doctor Strange
107 Captain Marvel
108 The Invincible Iron Man
110 The Big Freeze
111 Ratatouille
112 Aladdin
113 Aladdin - I am the Genie
114 Seven Dwarfs Find a House
115 Toy Story
116 Toy Story 4
117 Paw Patrol - Jurassic Bark!
118 Paw Patrol
- Mighty Pup Power!
121 The Lion King - I am Simba
122 Winnie the Pooh
- The Honey Tree
123 Frozen II
124 Baby Shark and the
Colours of the Ocean
125 Baby Shark and
the Police Sharks!
126 Trolls World Tour
127 I am Elsa
128 I am Anna
129 I am Olaf
130 I am Mulan
131 Sleeping Beauty
132 Onward
133 Paw Patrol
– Puppy Birthday to You!
134 Black Widow
135 Trolls – Poppy's Big Day!
136 Baby Shark and the Tooth Fairy
137 Baby Shark – Mummy Shark
138 Inside Out
139 The Prince and the Pauper
140 Finding Dory
142 The Lion King
- Simba's Daring Rescue

Book list may be subject to change. Not all titles are listed.